HAND LETTERED BY
SARAH KLINGER

enchantedlionbooks.com

First published in 2016 by Enchanted Lion Books
351 Van Brunt Street, Brooklyn, NY 11231
Originally published in French as *Mon Bébé Croco*
Mon Bébé Croco © 2015, Albin Michel Jeunesse
Copyright © 2016 by Enchanted Lion Books for the English-language translation
All rights reserved under International and Pan-American Copyright Conventions
A CIP record is on file with the Library of Congress
ISBN 978-1-59270-192-6

Printed in China

First Printing

MY BABY CROCODILE

—

GAËTAN DORÉMUS

TRANSLATED FROM THE FRENCH BY SARAH KLINGER

ENCHANTED LION BOOKS

NEW YORK

Airdrie Public Library
111 - 304 Main Street S
Airdrie, Alberta T4B 3C3

ONE DAY I'M OUT HUNTING
WHEN I FIND AN ABANDONED
BABY CROCODILE.

ODDLY, HE DOESN'T SEEM HUNGRY AND HE'S SHIVERING, EVEN THOUGH IT'S SUNNY.

NATURALLY, I TRY TO PROTECT HIM. WHEN HE WAKES UP, I'D DIG FOR A LITTLE SNACK.

WANT TO CURL UP AND FINISH YOUR NAP, LITTLE BABY? NO?

AS I RECALL, BABIES LIKE WARM BATHS. INTO THE WATER YOU GO!

SHOOT. MAYBE BABIES DON'T KNOW HOW TO SWIM.

AS USUAL, I BOB UP AND DOWN LIKE A LOG,
BUT HE'S STIFF AS A BOARD.

LOOK AT THAT—HE'S RUSTING!

AND HE DOESN'T SEEM TO LIKE THE BLANKET I GAVE HIM. I GUESS I DON'T KNOW MUCH ABOUT BABIES AFTER ALL.

TiME FOR A GOODNIGHT KISS...? YOU DON'T LIKE KISSES?

I'M YAWNING. IT MUST BE LATE. TIME FOR BED!

OFF HE GOES. HEY! YOU'RE NOT SLEEPY?

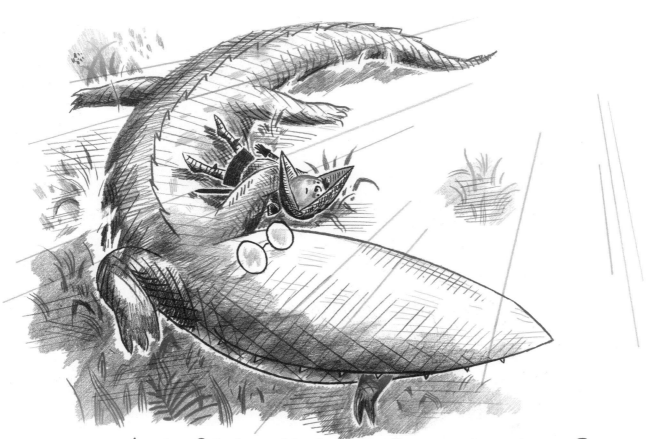

YOU'LL BE CRANKY IF YOU DON'T GET SOME REST.
COME ON, SNUGGLE UP. THERE NOW. SWEET DREAMS!
AND I'LL GLADLY GOBBLE UP YOUR BLANKET.

HE'LL GET SOME REST.

JUST AS I SUSPECTED, HE'S COMPLETELY TUCKERED OUT.
SO WHILE I LOOK FOR FOOD...

I'LL HAVE TO TEACH HIM SOME SURVIVAL SKILLS.
RULE N°1: YOU MUST LEARN TO SNEAK UP ON YOUR PREY.

DRAT, HE SHINES IN THE MOONLIGHT!
OUR DINNER IS ESCAPING.

UH-OH, NOW HE SQUEAKS WHEN HE WALKS BECAUSE OF THE MUD. THE ANIMALS ARE RUNNING AWAY.

I'LL JUST COVER HIM IN MUD SO HE WON'T BE SO SHINY. ALL RIGHT, THIS TIME, LET'S TRY TO STAY HIDDEN.

WELL, LOOK AT THAT! NOW OUR MEAL IS CHASING HIM.
HAHAHA, BABIES ARE SO FUNNY!

DINNNNERTIME! JUST LOOK AT THIS FEAST.
YOU'RE NOT HUNGRY?
YOU DON'T LIKE "RAW" MEAT?

WHAT'S "RAW," ANYWAY?
OH. NOT EVEN IF IT'S JUICY.?

IT'S MORNING AND WE'RE BOTH FALLING ASLEEP.
HE MAY BE A BIT DIFFERENT, BUT I'LL PROTECT HIM.
HE'S MY BABY AFTER ALL.

WHEN NIGHT FALLS, WE WAKE UP AND HE DOESN'T LOOK SO GOOD.
I CAN'T SEE ALL THAT WELL, BUT EVEN SO I CAN TELL HE'S GOT A FUNNY
LUMP IN HIS THROAT. I'LL MENTION IT TO THE DOCTOR.

BUT NOW IT'S PLAYTIME. IT'S GOOD FOR HIM TO MEET OTHER BABIES.

ONE RAINY NIGHT WHEN WE'RE OUT HUNTING AND HE'S DRAGGING BEHIND ME, SUDDENLY—BOOM! OH NO! MY BABY!

THANKFULLY, HE'S ALL RIGHT, AND I LEARN THREE THINGS: 1. HE ATTRACTS FIRE FROM THE SKY. 2. HE LIKES TO "COOK" HIS MEAT.

3. "COOKED" MEAT IS SCRUMPTIOUS.
WHAT A FUNNY BABY I HAVE...

I INVITE A FRIEND OVER TO TRY THE "COOKED" MEAT,
AND MY BABY GOES AND HIDES. HOW SHY HE IS!

Now he says he's cold,
so he snuggles up close.

It's all really strange.
He says he sleeps better high up in the trees and that
he's afraid of the dark and needs me to stay near him
because my glasses are like "nightlights."

IN THE AFTERNOONS HE COMPLAINS HE'S TOO HOT.
HE TELLS ME HE BAKES IN THE SUN.

SO I SUGGEST A COOL DIP IN THE RIVER,
JUST AS LONG AS HE DOESN'T WANDER OFF TOO FAR DURING MY NAP.
THEN I CHANGE MY MIND AND FOLLOW HIM, I DON'T KNOW WHY.

AND THERE I SEE HiM
TAKiNG OFF HIS SKiN...

WHAT...!!!

BUT THEN I DECIDE THAT THIS LITTLE BOY
WILL ALWAYS BE MY BABY.

He's not eating me.

Next, I make a fire.

We eat fish balls with fruit salad. Yum!

We play catch with a watermelon and it floats.

We play hide-and-seek. Without my shiny, squeaky armor, I'm really good.

I show him hunting traps.

He warns me about dangerous animals.

Then, as usual, my old cross-eyed crocodile takes his nap.

But me, I can't sleep.

I think. A lot.

When he wakes up, I tell him everything.
We give each other a big goodbye hug and then...

JUST KIDDING! Life in the wild
is way better than life inside a stuffy castle!

Come on!

It would be so easy to return home a hero.

But then, who would play with me?

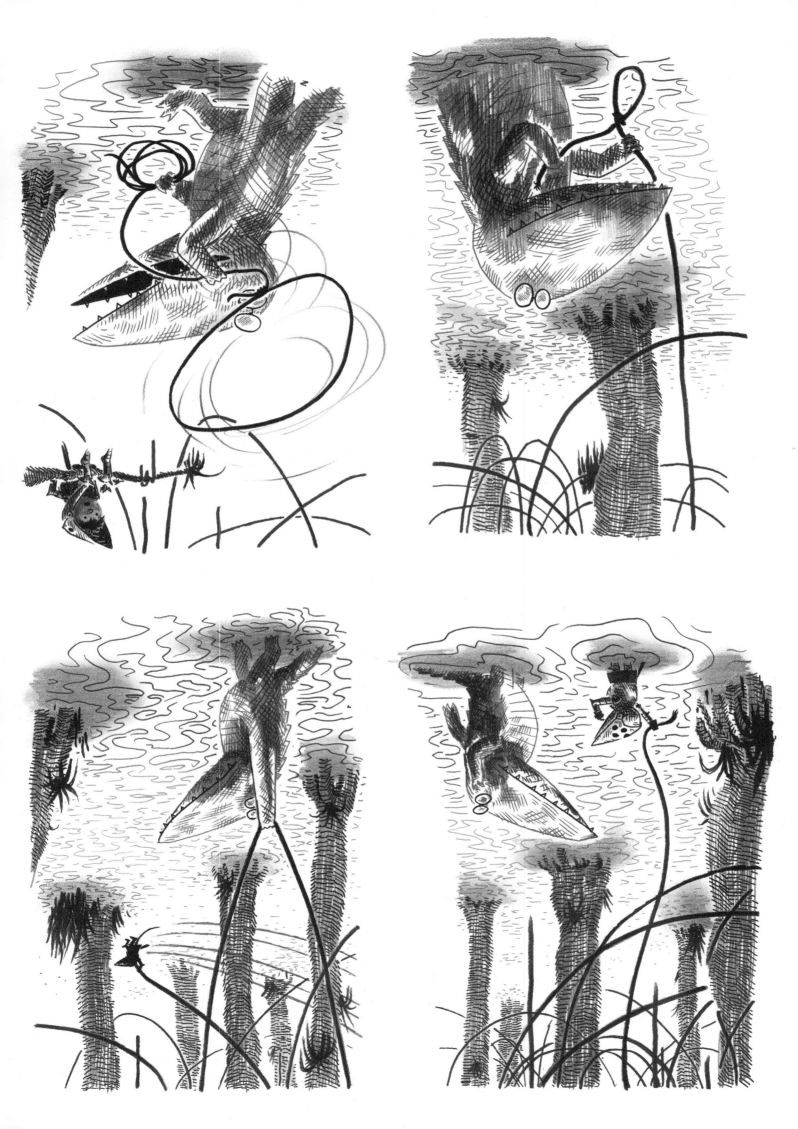

IT WOULD BE SO EASY TO GOBBLE HIM UP.

BUT THEN, I'D BE ALL ALONE WITH MY FULL BELLY.

No, I can't.

Still, I'm afraid to play blind man's bluff.

STILL, I'M AFRAID TO PLAY HIDE-AND-SEEK.

This way he won't bite me.

"YOU'D REALLY THREATEN ME WITH THE SWORD I SWIPED FROM YOU?" He scolds.

We give each other one last big hug.

AND GO OUR SEPARATE WAYS...

To live our lives. (WITHOUT LOOKING BACK.)

BABY CROCODILE!
Grandpa Crocodile!